Tea Party for Two

A Yearling First Choice Chapter Book

Tea Party for Two

Michelle Poploff

illustrated by
Maryann Cocca-Leffler

To Kathy, Ingrid, Sherri, and Wendy
Thanks for your friendship
—M.J.P.

To my friend,
Lucinda McQueen
—Love, M.C.L.

Published by
Bantam Doubleday Dell Publishing Group, Inc.
1540 Broadway
New York, New York 10036

Library of Congress Cataloging-in-Publication Data
Poploff, Michelle.
   Tea party for two / Michelle Poploff; illustrated by Maryann Cocca-
Leffler.
      p. cm.
   "A Yearling first choice chapter book."
   Summary: While Kim and Amy make one last trip inside the house before
beginning their outdoor tea party, Walter and the neighbor's dog eat up
all the food left in the backyard.
   ISBN 0-385-32260-7 (alk. paper). —ISBN 0-440-41334-6 (pbk.: alk. paper)
   [1. parties—Fiction.   2. Birthdays—Fiction.]   I. Cocca-Leffler, Maryann,
ill.   II. Title.
PZ7.P7959Te   1997
[E]—dc20   96-8329 CIP AC

Hardcover: The trademark Delacorte Press® is registered in the
U.S. Patent and Trademark Office and in other countries.
Paperback: The trademark Yearling® is registered in the
U.S. Patent and Trademark Office and in other countries.

The text of this book is set in 17-point Baskerville.
Book design by Trish Parcell Watts
Manufactured in the United States of America
November 1997
10 9 8 7 6 5 4 3 2 1

Contents

~1~
Special Delivery

Amy loved getting mail.

One day the mailman

gave her a pink envelope.

Her name was on it.

Inside was a card.

Let's have a tea party for two.
It will be just me and you.
From your best friend, Kim.
Teatime: Tuesday, 12 noon
Place: Kim's backyard

P.S. No brothers
or sisters allowed.

Amy called Kim on the telephone.

"I can come to the tea party," said Amy.

"But there's one problem."

"Uh-oh," said Kim. "What is it?"

"I don't like tea," said Amy.

"I always drink it when I'm sick. Yuck."

"We can't have a tea party
without tea," said Kim.

Amy didn't want to ruin their tea party.
"Let's have lemonade
and pretend it's lemon tea," said Amy.
"Then it will still be a tea party."
"Great idea," said Kim.
"See you tomorrow at noon."

-2-
Pink Strawberry Cupcakes

The next day was warm and sunny.

Amy's mother drove
her to Kim's house.

The girls went out
to the backyard.

"This is a do-it-yourself
tea party," said Kim.

"Let's see what we can find."

Inside the green shed they found
a red-and-white checkered tablecloth.

"We can use this for
our picnic blanket," Kim said.

They spread the plastic cloth
near a shady tree.
"Look at all those mustard and
ketchup stains," said Amy.
"We'll cover them
with flowers," said Kim.
The girls covered the spots
with daisies and sunflowers.

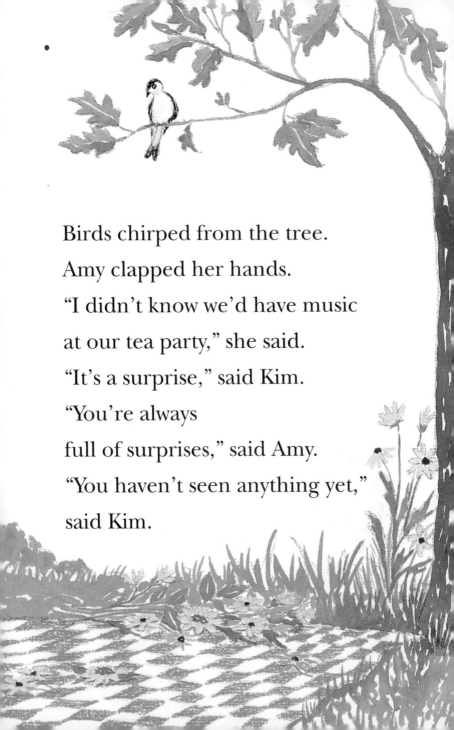

Birds chirped from the tree.
Amy clapped her hands.
"I didn't know we'd have music
at our tea party," she said.
"It's a surprise," said Kim.
"You're always
full of surprises," said Amy.
"You haven't seen anything yet,"
said Kim.

Kim went back to the shed.
She returned with
a white straw picnic basket.
It was a little dusty.
Amy blew dust off it.
Kim said, "I helped my mother
make crunchy peanut butter
and grape jelly sandwiches.
We cut off the crusts for you."

"I brought our favorite

strawberry cupcakes," said Amy.

"The ones with the lacy pink frosting."

"From Honey Bunch

Bakery Shop?" asked Kim.

"But of course," said Amy.

She brushed at her wavy bangs.

"They smelled so good.

I almost took a bite on the ride over."

"But you didn't," said Kim.

Amy shook her head.

"I just kept sniffing at them."

Kim licked her lips. "Thank goodness.

Come on," she said.

"Help me bring the food outside."

-3-
Stomach Gurgles

Kim and Amy unpacked
their tea party picnic.
They put the crunchy peanut butter
and grape jelly sandwiches
on the cloth.
Kim's had crusts.
Amy's did not.
Next came a teapot of lemonade.
Amy reached into the basket.
"I can't wait to try
these juicy green grapes," she said.
"No little seeds inside," said Kim.

They unwrapped the lacy pink
strawberry cupcakes.

"These are the best," said Kim.

"We'll save them for last."

"I can't wait another second," said Amy.

"Let's eat right now."

"We're not ready," Kim said.

"Says who?" said Amy.

"I'm ready, and so is my stomach.

Listen to this."

Kim bent her head down.

She heard Amy's stomach gurgle.

"Tell your stomach to wait," Kim said.
"We still need to bring my
little pink china cups and plates."
"You mean the tea party set you got
from your grandma?"
"Naturally," said Kim. "The best
surprise is the napkins I bought.
They have little pink teacups
on them."
"But can't I take
just one bite?" asked Amy.

Kim pulled Amy's arm.

"Not until we wash up," said Kim.

"It's our last trip inside."

Amy rubbed her stomach.

"Did you hear that?

One last trip. Little pink teacups.

Then it's really tea party time."

-4-
Hungry Jack Snack Attack

The girls walked into the kitchen.

"Stop poking fun at me," said Kim.

"You sound like my brother, Walter."

Amy's mouth dropped open.

"That little squirt," she said. "Never.

Where is he, anyway?"

"Down the block
playing with the
neighbor's dog,"
said Kim.

"I thought it was too peaceful
around here," said Amy.

Kim smiled. "It's perfect," she said.

The girls washed up at the kitchen sink.
"Where's the soap?" Amy asked.
"Let's use the dish lotion," said Kim.
Soon the water was soapy
and filled with bubbles.
Amy and Kim stuck their arms
in up to their elbows.
They put soapy suds on
each other's cheeks and chins.

They had so much fun they almost
forgot about their tea party.

While Amy blew bubbles at Kim,
Kim's little brother, Walter,
marched into their backyard.
The neighbor's big, black, hairy mutt,
Hungry Jack, trotted beside him.
"Look at these great snacks,
Hungry Jack," said Walter.
"It's like magic."
He took a bite out of one
strawberry cupcake.
He licked the
lacy pink top.
"But it's real.

I bet Kim had a picnic.
These are leftovers, right, boy?"
Hungry Jack yelped.
"I think so too.
We'll share."
Hungry Jack wagged his tail.

"This is a great birthday surprise
for you. All I had to give you
was a hunk of salami.
I'm sure glad Kim left this for us."
Walter carefully split the cupcakes
and sandwiches with Hungry Jack.

Walter ate all the grapes.

"Good, no seeds. My favorites."

Hungry Jack lapped up the lemonade.

"I have a great sister,"

Walter said to Hungry Jack.

"I wonder where she is, anyway?"

-5-
Super-duper Party Pooper

Amy popped the very last bubble
on Kim's nose.

"That was fun," said Amy.

"Our hands are squeaky clean.

Now can we please eat?"

Kim nodded.

They quickly packed
the tea party cups, plates, and napkins.

Amy grabbed the basket
and ran out the door.

After a few steps, she stopped.

Kim bumped into Amy.

She clapped her hand over her mouth.

"Oh my gosh!
What happened
to our tea party?" said Kim.

Amy ran to the checkered tablecloth.

The basket swung on her arm.

"Don't break my dishes," Kim called.

Amy set the basket on the grass.

"What do you think you're doing?"

Kim asked her brother.

"Eating your leftovers," said Walter.

There was pink icing on his front teeth.

A gob of peanut butter

dangled from Hungry Jack's chin.

"Those weren't leftovers," said Amy.

"That was our tea party food."

Walter looked from Kim to Amy.

He smacked his lips.
"Now I get it," he said.
"Too bad my stomach
doesn't get it," said Amy.

"You ruined our tea party," said Kim.

"We didn't mean to," said Walter.

Walter put his arm around

Hungry Jack's neck.

"We thought this was a

surprise birthday party."

"Don't tell me

it's your birthday," said Amy.

"It's Hungry Jack's," said Walter.

"He's three years old today.

That's twenty-one in dog years."

Amy turned to Kim.

"Your invitation said a

tea party for two," said Amy.

She pointed at Walter and Jack.

"I didn't think it meant those two."

"It's okay," said Walter.

"What's okay?" the girls asked.

"It's okay that you didn't
bring Hungry Jack a present."

"We didn't know it
was his birthday," said Amy.

"That's why it's
a surprise party," said Walter.

"And it's been swell.

But I have to go.

It's Hungry Jack's naptime."

"Not so fast." Kim grabbed Walter's arm.
"Hold still, you super-duper
party pooper," Amy said.
She grabbed Walter's other arm.

"Wait until *your* friends
come over," said Kim.
"I'll tell them you suck your toes."
"Do not," said Walter.
"Do too."
Walter stomped his foot.
"Tattletale," he said.
"Toe sucker," said Kim.
Walter stuck out his bottom lip.
"Woof, woof," barked Hungry Jack.
"Give me one more chance,"
said Walter. "I'll do anything."

~6~
Party Pals

"What will you do?" asked Amy.

"Don't ask," said Kim.

"You can't win with Walter."

Hungry Jack sneezed.

Wet spray covered the girls.

"Gross," said Amy.

"We just washed up.

And I'm still starving."

"Here's my chance," Walter said.

"Wait right there."

He ran into the house and
brought out half a salami.
"I saved this for Hungry Jack.
But you can eat it now."
Amy stuck out her tongue. "No way."
"We're not eating salami
at a tea party, Walter," Kim said.
"I can't think of anything
else to do," said Walter.

"I can," said Kim.
She folded her arms
across her chest.
"Oh, all right," said Walter.
"We're sorry we messed
up your party. Right, pal?"
Hungry Jack wagged his tail.

Finally, Kim winked at Amy.
"At least Hungry Jack had
a good party," she said.
Amy winked back. "There are still
two cupcakes in the box on the table."

Kim nodded. "And there's iced tea
in the fridge," she said.
"I bet you'll like it, Amy."
"Tea party, here we come," said Amy.
She reached for the basket.

"Before you go, let's sing
'Happy Birthday' to Hungry Jack,"
said Walter.

The girls looked at each other.

"We might as well," Kim said.

Kim, Amy, and Walter sang.

The birds tweeted from the trees.

Hungry Jack barked off-key.

"Thanks," said Walter.

Amy and Kim linked arms.

"Anything else, Walter?" asked Kim.

Walter burped softly.

Then he grinned.

"Next time let's have
chocolate cupcakes."

Michelle Poploff is the author of the Busy O'Brien books, including *Busy O'Brien and the Great Bubble Gum Blowout* and *Busy O'Brien and the Caterpillar Punch Bunch,* as well as *Splash-a-Roo and Snowflakes,* illustrated by Diane Palmisciano. Michelle Poploff lives in New York City with her husband, Jeff, and their children, Daniel and Leanne.

Maryann Cocca-Leffler has illustrated many books for children, including *Clams All Year* and *Wednesday Is Spaghetti Day,* both of which she wrote. She lives in New England with her husband, Eric, and two daughters, Janine and Kristin.